For Violet Nymphadora

WE CATCH THE BUS

KATIE ABEY

BLOOMSBURY
CHILDREN'S BOOKS
LONDON OXFORD NEW YORK NEW DELHI SYDNEY

We Catch the Bus

Which bus would you catch?

We Ride Tractors

What are the animals **doing** on the farm?

Moving logs

Ploughing soil

Cutting the grass

Camping

Who is hiding in the pond?

My vehicle is red

I ♥ tractors

We Fly Rockets

The animals have blasted off! What will they **find** in space?